35 Kilos of Hope

35 Kilos of Hope

Anna Gavalda

WALKER BOOKS
AND SUBSIDIARIES

LONDON · BOSTON · SYDNEY · AUCKLAND

This edition first published
in Great Britain 2004 by Walker Books Ltd
87 Vauxhall Walk, London SE11 5HJ

First published in France by Bayard Éditions Jeunesse, 2002,
under the title *35 kilos d'espoir*

Published by arrangement with Viking Children's Books,
a division of Penguin Group (USA) Inc.

Cover photograph by Donna Day/Getty Images
Cover design by Walker Books Ltd

2 4 6 8 10 9 7 5 3 1

This book has been typeset in Melior Educational

Printed and bound in Great Britain
by Cox & Wyman Ltd, Reading, Berkshire

British Library Cataloguing in Publication Data:
a catalogue record for this book is
available from the British Library

ISBN 1-84428-652-5

www.walkerbooks.co.uk

To my Grandpa
and to Marie Tondelier

1

I hate school.

I hate it more than anything in the world.

And even worse than that...

It's ruining my life.

Until I was three, I'd say my life was happy. I don't really remember that much, but I think things were OK. I would spend my time playing, watching my Little Brown Bear video over and over again, drawing pictures and making up hundreds of adventures starring Big Doggy, the stuffed dog I adored. My mum told me that I used to spend hours in my room giggling and chatting away to myself. So I suppose I must have been happy.

At that time in my life, I loved everyone and I thought everyone loved me. Then, when I was four years old, *wham!*

School.

Apparently, in the morning, I was quite happy to go. My parents must have gone on about it all through the summer: *Who's a lucky boy, going to big school...? Look at this lovely new schoolbag! It's for your lovely new school!* And blah blah blah.

Apparently, I didn't even cry. (I'm

the curious type. I think I wanted to see what kind of toys they had, especially Lego.)

Apparently, when I came home at lunchtime I was very excited. When I'd eaten, I went into my room to tell Big Doggy all about my marvellous morning.

Well, if only I'd known, I would've paid more attention to those last minutes of happiness, because straight after that my life went right off the rails.

"Time to go back," said Mum.

"Where to?"

"To school, of course!"

"No."

"No what?"

"No, I'm not going."

"Oh? And why not?"

"Because I've already been. I've seen what it's like, and it's not interesting. I've got lots of things to do in my room. I told Big Doggy I was going to build him a special machine for finding all the bones he's buried under my bed, so I haven't got time for school."

My mum knelt down beside me, and I shook my head.

She spoke more firmly, and I started to cry.

She picked me up and I started to scream.

Then she smacked me.

It was the first smack of my life.

There you are.

That was school for you.

The beginning of the nightmare.

I've heard my parents tell this story a million times. They've told their friends, my infant-school teachers, my junior-school teachers, psychologists, speech therapists and careers advisors. And each time I hear it, I remember that I never did build that bone detector for Big Doggy.

Now I'm thirteen, and I'm in year seven. Yes, I know there's something wrong here. Don't bother to count on your fingers, I'll tell you what it is straight away. I got kept back twice in my last school.

School always causes scenes at

home. You can imagine... My mum cries and my dad yells – or the other way round, my mum yells and my dad says nothing. It drives me mad to see them like that, but what can I do? What can I say? Nothing. I say nothing, because if I open my mouth, it's even worse. There's only one thing the two of them ever say to me, and they repeat it like a couple of demented parrots:

"Work!"

"Work! Work! Work!"

"Work!"

OK, I understand. I'm not a complete moron. I would *like* to work; the problem is, I can't. For me, it's like they teach everything in Chinese. It goes in one ear and out the other. They've taken me to *thousands* of doctors: eye doctors, ear doctors, head doctors. Their conclusion after all these hours of consultation? I've got a concentration problem.

ADD.

Attention Deficit Disorder.

You've got to be joking! I know exactly what's wrong, and it's got nothing to do with a concentration problem. I haven't *got* a problem. Not a single one. It's just that school doesn't interest me.

It doesn't interest me in the least, and that's all there is to it.

There was just one year when I was happy at school. It was my second year of infant school with a teacher named Marie. I'll never forget her.

When I think about it now, I tell myself that Marie must have become an infant teacher so she could spend her time doing what she liked best in life: building and creating things. I loved her from the beginning. From the first morning of the first day. She wore clothes that she'd made herself, jumpers that she'd knitted herself, and her jewellery was all her own work. Not a day went by when we didn't take something home: a papier mâché hedgehog, a milk-bottle cat, a mouse in a walnut shell; mobiles, drawings, paintings, collages... Marie didn't wait till Mother's Day for us to get our hands dirty. She would say that a successful day was a day when you made something.

Sometimes I wonder if the happiness of that year with Marie was also the reason for the misery that followed, because it was then that I realized a simple truth: nothing interested me much except my own hands and what I could make with them.

But I also know what I owe Marie. Thanks to her, I managed to get through infant school reasonably well. She understood what made me tick. She knew that having to write my name brought me to the verge of tears, that I found it hard to take things in, that, for me, reciting a nursery rhyme was pure torture. At the end of the year, on the last day, I went to say goodbye to her. I had a lump in my throat and could hardly talk. I handed her my present. It was a clever little pencil box with one drawer for paper clips, another for drawing pins, a place for the rubber and everything. It'd taken me hours to get it right. I saw that she liked it, and that she felt as emotional as I did.

"I've got a present for you too, Gregory," she said. It was a big fat book. "Next year you'll be in Mrs Daret's class. You're going to have to try very hard ... d'you know why?"

I shook my head.

"So you'll be able to read everything that's in here."

When I got home, I asked my mum to read me the title. She took the huge volume on her knee and said, "*One Thousand Things for Little Hands to*

Do. My goodness, I can see the mess already!"

I hated Mrs Daret. I hated the sound of her voice, the way she bossed us about, and the fact that she always had favourites. But I did learn to read, because I wanted to make the egg-carton hippopotamus on page 124 of *One Thousand Things for Little Hands to Do.*

On my final report from infant school Marie wrote: "This boy has a head like a sieve, magic fingers and a heart of gold. We should be able to make something of him."

It was the first and last time in my life that I received a compliment from a member of the national education system.

2

Anyway, I know plenty of people who don't like school. You, for example. If I ask "Do you like school?" you'll laugh and tell me not to ask stupid questions. Only total crawlers would say yes, or the ones who are so clever that it's like a game for them to test out their brainpower every morning. Otherwise, who really likes it? Nobody. And who really hates it? Not that many either. Except the ones like me, the ones they call stupid, the ones who get sick to their stomachs.

I open my eyes at least an hour before the alarm goes off, and for that hour I feel the knot swelling up in my stomach. When I get up, I feel so sick it's like being on a boat on the high seas. Breakfast is torture. In fact, I can't swallow a mouthful, but since my mum is always standing over me I take a couple of dry biscuits. On the bus my stomach ache turns into a hard stone. If I meet friends and we start talking about Tomb Raider or something, I feel a bit better and the stone gets lighter; but if I'm alone, it chokes me. The worst moment of all is when I arrive at the school door. It's the *smell* of school that makes me sick. The years go by and the places change, but that smell stays the same. That mixture of chalk and old trainers, it grabs me by the throat and makes me gag.

The stone starts melting away around four o'clock, and by the time I get back to my bedroom it's completely dissolved. It comes back when my parents get home and start asking me about my day and rifling through my schoolbag to check out my homework book. But with them the pain is not so strong, because I'm used to their little scenes.

Well, not exactly. I'm not telling the truth here. I can't get used to them. Fight after fight, and I still can't stand it. *I can't stand it.* Since my parents don't love each other that much any more, they need to have a fight every evening;

and because they don't know how to get started, they use me and my bad marks as an excuse. They blame everything on that. Then my mum blames my dad for never having taken the time to do things with me, and my dad says it's all her fault for spoiling me rotten.

And I'm fed up, I'm so fed up.

I'm more fed up than you could ever imagine.

When it's like that, I block my ears from the inside and I concentrate on what I'm building: a Lego spaceship for Anakin Skywalker, or a Meccano gadget for squeezing toothpaste tubes. Then comes the torture of homework. If my mum helps me, she always ends up crying. If it's my dad, I always end up crying.

I'm telling you all this, but I wouldn't want you to think I've got terrible parents, or that they take things out on me. It's not that at all. My parents are great. Well ... sort of. I mean, they're just *normal*. It's school that ruins everything. Last year I only wrote down half the homework we were given in my notebook. I did it to avoid all those evenings of misery. That was the only reason, but I didn't dare say so to the headmistress the day I found myself in her office in tears. Stupid really.

Anyway, it was just as well I kept quiet. Would that fat old turkey have understood? Obviously not, because the following month she expelled me.

She expelled me because of PE.

I have to say, I hate PE almost as

much as I hate school. Not quite as much, but *nearly*. If you could see me, you'd understand why me and judo mats don't go together. I'm not very tall, not very co-ordinated and not very strong. I'll go further: I'm not very tall, not very co-ordinated, and I've got the muscles of a teddy bear.

Sometimes I stand in front of the mirror with my hands on my hips, puffing out my chest. It's a sorry sight. I look like a worm doing body building, or like Popeye before he eats his spinach.

But I can't let everything in life get me down. Something's got to give, otherwise I'd go completely mad. And the something that gave last year was PE. Even writing these words makes me smile. Mrs Berry and her PE class were always good for a laugh.

This is how it began.

"Murray, Gregory," she said, eyeing her clipboard.

"Yes?"

I knew that yet again I would mess up the gym routine and look ridiculous. I wondered when it would all end.

I stepped forward. The others were already beginning to snigger.

But for once they weren't laughing at my feeble performance. They were laughing at how I looked. I'd forgotten my gym stuff, and since it was the third time that term, I'd borrowed Ben's brother's kit to avoid another detention. (I've had more detentions in one

year than you'll get in your entire life.)
What I hadn't realized was that Ben's
brother was six foot tall and three foot
wide.

So there I was flapping about in an
XXL tracksuit and size-ten trainers.
Needless to say, I was an instant hit.

"What on earth are you wearing?"
yelled Berry.

I put on my innocent look and said,
"I just can't understand it, Mrs Berry.
Last week it fitted perfectly..."

She looked like she was about to
explode. "Double somersault, feet
together, NOW!"

I did one catastrophic somersault
and lost a trainer. I heard the others
laughing, so to entertain them I did
another one, and managed to send my

other shoe flying towards the ceiling.

When I got up, my underpants were showing because my tracksuit bottoms had slipped down. Mrs Berry was bright red, and my classmates were cracking up. The sound of that laughter made me feel good — for once I wasn't being made fun of. This was laughter like you hear at the circus, and from that moment on I decided to be the PE class clown. Mrs Berry's court jester. Making people laugh gives you a warm feeling inside. It's like a drug; the more people laugh, the more you want to make them.

Mrs Berry gave me so many detentions that there was no more room in my school report book, but I don't regret it. Thanks to her, I did feel a tiny bit happy at school, just a tiny bit useful.

I have to admit, I caused absolute chaos. Before, no one wanted me on their team because I was so pathetic, but afterwards they fought over me because my pranks put the opposing team off their game. I remember one day when they put me in as goalie ... what a scono! When the ball came towards me, I shimmied up the net of the goal like a panic-stricken monkey, squealing in terror, and when I had to put the ball back in the game, I always managed to throw it the wrong way and score an own goal.

At one point I lunged forward to grab the ball. Of course, I didn't get near enough to touch it, but when I got up I was munching a tuft of grass, mooing like a cow. That was the day Katy Lynch peed her pants, and I got a two-hour detention. But hey, it was worth it!

I was expelled because of the horse. Actually, it's sort of ironic, because for once I wasn't messing around. We had to jump onto this huge foam rubber thing, grabbing hold of the handles. When my turn came I missed and really hurt my ... well, you know what I mean. My willy was crushed to a pulp. Of course, everyone thought I'd done it on purpose, that I was faking the *Yeeowww!* to make them laugh. Berry dragged me straight to the head-mistress's office. I was doubled up in agony, but I didn't cry.

I didn't want to give them the satisfaction.

My parents didn't believe me either, and when they heard I'd been expelled they went berserk. For once they were screaming in harmony, and they certainly put their hearts into it.

When they finally let me go back to my room, I shut the door and sat on the floor. I told myself: "Either you climb into bed and cry – and you'd be right to cry because your life is worth nothing, and neither are you, so you might as well curl up and die right now – or you get up and make something."

That evening, I constructed a giant monster out of a load of old scraps I'd found on a building site and called it Hairy Berry after my favourite PE teacher. Not the best joke in the world, I admit, but it did me good, and at least it kept my pillow dry.

3

The only person who was any comfort to me in those days was my grandad. Which isn't surprising, because Grandad Leo had always been the one who made me feel better — ever since I was old enough to go into his workshop.

Grandad Leo's workshop was my life. It was my hideout, my Aladdin's cave. When my gran started getting on our nerves, Grandad would wink at me and whisper, "Gregory, how would you like a little trip to Leoland?"

And we'd tiptoe off while my gran grumbled, "Go on then! Fill the child's head with nonsense!"

He would shrug his shoulders, and reply, "Please, Charlotte, please – Gregory and I need a bit of peace to think."

"To think about what, if it's not asking too much?"

"I think about my past, and Gregory thinks about his future."

My gran would turn her back on him saying that she'd rather go deaf than listen to such rubbish. And Grandad Leo always replied, "But sweetheart, you already are deaf."

Grandad Leo is good with his hands like I am, but he's clever too. When he

was at school he was a real star –
always top of the class, even though he
told me that he'd never studied on
Sundays. ("Why? Because I didn't feel
like it, that's why.") He came top in
maths, French, Latin, English, history,
everything! When he was eighteen he
got into the hardest university in the
country. After that, he designed huge
projects: bridges, motorways, tunnels,
dams. Whenever I asked him exactly
what he did, he would relight his
cigarette and think out loud.

"I don't know. I have never known
the precise definition of my job... Let's
just say that they would ask me to
look over plans and tell them what I
thought: was the thing in question
about to fall apart, yes or no?"

"Is that all?"

"Is that all, is that all...? It's important you know. If you say no and the bridge falls down just the same, you feel a real idiot, believe me!"

My grandad's workshop is the place where I'm happiest in the world. It's not much; just a shed in the backyard made of planks and corrugated iron. It's too cold in winter and too hot in summer. But I go there as often as I can. To make things, to borrow tools or bits of wood, and to see Grandad Leo at work (at the moment he's making a sideboard for a restaurant). I go to ask his advice, or for no reason at all. Just because I like being in a place that feels right. You know I told you about the smell of school that makes me feel

like throwing up? Well, in the workshop it's the opposite. When I'm in
that overcrowded shack, I breathe in
deeply and smell happiness. It's the
smell of oil, grease, the electric heater,
the soldering iron, putty, tobacco and
all the rest. It's delicious. I promise
myself that one day I'll find a way
to distil it, and invent a perfume
callod "Eau de Workshop". Then I can
breathe it in whenever life gets me
down.

When Grandad Leo found out that I
was staying down in year three, he took
me on his lap and told me the story of
the hare and the tortoise. I remember
exactly how I snuggled up to him, and
how soft his voice was.

"You see, nobody bet a penny on

that pathetic tortoise, she was far too slow. But in the end she won the race. And do you know how she did it? She did it because she was a brave little tortoise who never gave up. Like you, Toto: you are brave and determined too... I know that, because I've seen you at work. I've seen you spend hours and hours in the freezing cold, sandpapering some scrap of wood or painting one of your models. I think you're just like that tortoise."

"But they never ask us to do sandpapering at school!" I sobbed in reply. "They only ask us to do impossible stuff!"

When Grandad Leo found out that I was being kept down in year six, it was a different story.

I arrived at their house as usual, but he didn't answer when I said hello. We ate in silence, and after coffee he made no sign of moving.

"Grandad Leo?"

"What?"

"Shall we go to the workshop?"

"No."

"Why not?"

"Because your mother told me the bad news. I don't understand it, Gregory. You hate school, yet you do everything you can to stay there as long as possible."

I didn't reply.

"But you're not as stupid as they say. Or are you?"

His voice was hard.

"Yes I am."

"Pathetic! It's easy to say you're no good and do nothing! Of course – it's just fate, isn't it? So what next? What are you going to do now? Stay down over and over again, and with a bit of luck you'll get to college by the time you're thirty?"

I fiddled with the corner of a cushion, not daring to look up and meet his eyes.

"No, honestly, I just don't understand you, Gregory. So don't count on good old Leo any more. I like people who take their life into their own hands. I can't stand lazy people who wallow in self pity and get themselves expelled because they don't know how to behave. It doesn't make sense. Expelled and staying down. Good for you! Congratulations!

"When I think how I've always been on your side... Always! I told your parents to have faith in you, I made excuses for you, I encouraged you! I'll tell you this, my friend: it's easier to be unhappy than happy in this life, and I don't like people who take the easy way out. Be *happy*, for Pete's sake! Just do what you have to do to be happy!"

It was then that he started coughing. My gran came running, and I went outside.

I went into the workshop. I was freezing. I sat down on an old oil drum and wondered what I could do to take my life into my own hands.

If I could spend all my time building things I'd be happy, but there was a problem – I had no idea where to start.

No plans, no models, no materials, nothing. All I had was this huge pressure inside, which kept the tears from flowing.

I carved two words into my grandad's bench with my penknife and went home without saying goodbye.

4

At home, the crisis went on for longer and was even more agonizing than usual. It was the end of June and no school was prepared to take me in September. My parents were racking their brains and tearing their hair out. As for me, I shrank a little further into myself with each day that passed. I told myself that if I became small enough not to be noticed, I might even disappear completely, and all my problems would vanish with me.

I had been expelled on 11 June. At first, I hung around the house all day. In the morning, I'd watch chat shows or QVC (can you believe the stuff they sell on there?), and in the afternoon I re-read old comic books or worked on a 5000-piece jigsaw puzzle that Aunt Suzie had given me.

But I soon got bored. I had to find something to do with my hands. So I started looking around the house to see if there was anything I could improve. I'd often heard my mother moaning about the ironing, saying that she dreamt of being able to do it sitting down. I decided to attack the problem.

I unscrewed the base of the ironing board, the part that stopped Mum from being able to put her legs under it. I calculated the height and attached the board to four wooden legs like a normal desk. Then I took the wheels off an old shopping trolley that I'd found on the pavement the week before and fixed them onto a chair we didn't use any more. I even adapted the iron rest for the new iron she'd just bought. The whole job took me two days.

Next I dealt with the broken lawn-mower. I took the motor apart, cleaned it and put all the bits back together. It worked first time. My dad hadn't believed me, but I knew it wasn't worth taking it back to the garden centre. All it needed was a good clean.

That evening at dinner, the atmosphere was less stormy. To thank me,

Mum made my favourite thing, toasted cheese sandwiches, and Dad didn't turn the TV on.

He was the first to speak.

"You know, son, the sad thing about you is that you *do* have talent... So what can we do to help? You don't like school, we know. But school is compulsory till you're sixteen."

I nodded.

"It's a vicious circle: the less you work, the more you hate school; the more you hate school, the less you work... What are you going to do?"

"Wait till I'm sixteen, then get a job."

"Get real, Gregory! Who on earth would employ you?"

"No one, I know, but I'll invent

things, I'll make things. I don't need much money to live on."

"That's what you think. Of course you don't have to be rich, but you'll still need to buy tools, a workshop, a truck and all sorts of other stuff. But never mind. For the moment, let's not worry about money. That's not what bothers me. Let's talk about school. Gregory, don't make that face. Look at me, please. You won't get anywhere without a minimum of education. Imagine you invented some fantastic gadget. You'd have to take out a patent, wouldn't you? So you'd have to be able to write it up properly. And anyway, you can't just turn up at some company with your invention – you'd have to draw up plans, done to scale with accurate measurements, if you wanted to be taken seriously. Otherwise someone else would steal your idea before you could say *eureka!*"

"D'you think so?"

"I don't think so, I know so."

This bothered me; somehow, in all my confusion, I felt that he was right.

"But Dad, I've got one ... an invention that could make me seriously rich, even you maybe..."

"What is it?" asked my mum with a smile.

"Promise to keep it top secret?"

"Yes," they said together.

"Swear?"

"I swear."

"Me too."

"No, Mum, say 'I swear'."

"Oh – I swear."

"Well, it's this... Shoes specially made for people who go hiking in the mountains. These shoes have a little adjustable heel. You put it in normal position while you're going uphill, you take it off on level ground, and you put it under your toes to go downhill. That way your feet are always well balanced, and hill climbing isn't so hard."

My parents nodded in approval.

"It's a good idea, Gregory," said Mum. "You should get in touch with a sports shop like Decathlon."

I was pleased that they seemed to be taking me seriously. But the spell was broken when Dad chipped in.

"But if you want to *sell* this marvellous invention of yours, you'll have to be good at maths, at IT and economics. You see, we're back where we started. It's what I was saying before…"

Until the end of June I kept myself busy doing odd jobs. I helped our new neighbours to do their garden. I pulled up so many weeds that my fingers turned green and swollen. My hands looked like they belonged to the Incredible Hulk.

Our neighbours were Mr and Mrs Martin. They had a son called Charles who was only a year older than me. But we didn't get on. He was always stuck in front of his PlayStation or watching videos, and every time I saw him he asked me what class I'd be in next year. Which was more than a little irritating.

Mum continued to ring round trying to find a school that would take me in September. Every morning we received a stack of prospectuses in the post – swish photos on glossy paper boasting the merits of this or that school or college.

They were all completely fake. I leafed through them, shaking my head, wondering how they'd managed to get photos of the pupils smiling. Either it was bribery or the kids were being told that their teacher had just fallen off a cliff. There was only one school I liked the look of, but it was too far away, somewhere near Wales. In the photos the pupils weren't sitting behind desks smiling idiotically. They were in a greenhouse potting plants, or standing at a workbench sawing planks of wood. These students weren't smiling – they were concentrating. It didn't look bad, but it was a technical college. They'd never let me in. My stomach cramps returned without warning.

Mr Martin made me an offer: he would pay me to help him remove his old wallpaper. I accepted. We went to the tool shop and hired two steam wallpaper strippers. Charles and Mrs Martin had gone on holiday and my parents were working, so we were left in peace.

We did a good job, but it was pretty hard going. We were in the middle of a heatwave, and you can imagine what it's like being stuck in a steam bath when it's 25° in the shade... I drank lager for the first time. Disgusting.

Grandad Leo came by to give us a hand. Mr Martin was delighted. He said, "We are mere labourers, but you are a true artist Mr Murray." So my grandad pottered around revelling in the subtleties of plumbing and wiring while we sweated it out, swearing our heads off.

Mr Martin often said, "Damnus damna damnum damnorum damnis damnis." (It's Latin.)

Finally, my parents got me a place at the school just near our house. At first they didn't want to send me there because it had a bad reputation. The results were terrible and the students got mugged for their trainers, but since it was the only place that would take me, they didn't have much choice.

July flew past. I learned to paper walls: how to apply the paste and fold the sections of paper properly; how to smooth down the edges with the roller to get rid of air bubbles. I learned a lot of things. To this day, I'm ace at wall-papering with striped paper.

I also helped my grandad untangle the wiring and try out the electricity.

"Does it work?"

"No."

"And now?"

"No."

"Damn. And now?"

"Yes."

I made giant sandwiches, I varnished doors, changed fuses and listened to comedy shows on the radio for a whole month. A whole month of happiness.

It should have gone on for ever. In September I could have started another job with another boss... I thought of that as I tore into my salami sandwich; only three years left, and here I come.

But three years is a long time.

And there was another thing that worried me. Grandad Leo's health. He coughed more and more often and for longer and longer. He would sit down after the slightest exertion. My gran had made me promise to stop him from smoking, but I couldn't do it. He would say, "Leave me my one pleasure, Toto. I'll be dead soon enough."

This kind of answer made me furious.

"That's rubbish, *Toto*. You'll be dead soon *because* of your one pleasure!"

He laughed. "Since when did you get to call me *Toto*, Toto?"

When he smiled at me like that, I remembered he was the person I loved most in the world, and that he had no right to die. Ever.

The last day of the wallpapering job, Mr Martin took me and Grandad to a restaurant. They smoked a giant cigar each after the coffee. I couldn't bear to think of how my poor gran would've tortured herself with worry if she'd seen them.

As we were about to go our separate ways, my neighbour handed me an envelope.

"Here, take this. You've earned it."

I didn't open it straight away. I waited

till I was back home and opened it on my bed. A hundred quid! Five crisp twenties. I was absolutely stunned. I'd never even *seen* so much money, let alone had it in my possession. I didn't want to tell my parents because they would've gone on and on about how I should put it safely into my savings account. I wanted to hide the notes where no one in the world would find them. I racked my brains. I thought and thought and thought.

What was I going to buy with all that money? Motors for my models? Fifty comics? A CD-ROM called *One Hundred Incredible Constructions*? A leather jacket? A Bosch chainsaw?

Those five bank notes made my head spin, and when we went off on holiday in August I spent over an hour looking for a safe enough hiding place. I was just like my mother, running around with her great aunt's silver candlesticks.

I think we were both being pretty ridiculous.

5

There's nothing much to say about that August. Only that it was long and boring. Just like every year, my parents had rented a place in Brittany, and, just like every year, I had to slog through pages of exercises in my revision book. *Passport to Year Seven.* Take two.

I spent hours chewing the end of my pen, watching the seagulls. I dreamt that I turned into a seagull and flew as far as the red and white lighthouse on the horizon. I dreamt that I made friends with a swallow and in September – 4 September for example, which just happened to be the day school started up again – we left together for the sunny south. I dreamt that I crossed oceans, that we were flying...

Then I shook myself back into reality. I re-read my maths problem, some pointless story about sackfuls of plaster, and suddenly I was off in my dream again; a seagull made a direct hit on the problem... *Wham!* A big white splotch across the whole page. Problem solved.

I dreamt of all I could do with seven sackfuls of plaster.

In other words, I dreamt away my day.

My parents didn't look too closely at

my revision. After all, they were on holiday too, and they didn't want to stress themselves out trying to decipher my spidery scrawl. All they asked me to do was stay indoors every morning and spend the time sitting behind a desk.

It was all so meaningless. I covered the pages of that stupid revision book with drawings, sketches and crazy plans. I wasn't bored; it was just that my life didn't interest me. I asked myself: What difference does it make where I am? I also asked: To be or not to be, what does it matter? (As you can see, I may not be a mathematician, but I'm a bit of a philosopher.)

In the afternoons I would go to the beach with either my mum or my dad, never with both together. That was also part of their holiday arrangement; they were not obliged to put up with each other all day long. Things were not too good between my parents. Their words had double meanings, their remarks were loaded, and they snapped at each other constantly — all of which landed us in awkward silences. Our family was always in a bad mood. I dreamt of having a family like in the adverts, where everyone laughs and jokes at the breakfast table. But I was under no illusion.

When the time came for us to pack our bags and clear out of the house, a feeling of relief filled the air. It was madness. Spending a fortune to go so far away, just to be relieved to go home. I thought it was insane.

6

My mum got her candlesticks back, and I got my money. (Now I can tell you – I'd rolled the notes up and stuffed them into the barrel of my old Action Man gun.)

The leaves turned yellow, and my stomach turned over.

It was time for me to start at my new school.

I wasn't the oldest in the class, and I was far from being the worst. I gave myself a break. I stayed at the back and avoided the headcases. I gave up the idea of buying a leather jacket, because I was sure I wouldn't hold onto it for long in that place.

School no longer made me sick. The reason was simple; I didn't feel like I was at a school any more. I felt more like I was in a sort of zoo-cum-day-care-centre, where two thousand adolescents were left to their own devices from morning till night. I was a permanent vegetable. I was shocked at how some of the students spoke to the teachers. I made myself as inconspicuous as possible. Just counting the days.

In mid-October my mother suddenly went berserk. She couldn't stand the fact that I still hadn't even seen my language teacher. She also couldn't stand my vocabulary, and said that every day I got worse and worse, that I was getting to be like an animal. She couldn't understand why I was never given any marks for my work, and one day she went hysterical when she came to pick me up and saw kids my age hanging around outside the shopping arcade smoking joints.

The result was a mega-crisis at home. Screams, tears and much blowing of noses.

The upshot: boarding school.

After an evening of fighting, my parents finally agreed on one thing: I was going to boarding school.

Great.

I gritted my teeth.

*   *   *

The next day was Wednesday. I went to my grandparents'. My gran had made my favourite fried potatoes, and Grandad Leo didn't dare speak to me. The atmosphere was miserable.

After coffee, we went into his workshop. Grandad put an unlit cigarette between his lips.

"I'm giving up," he admitted. "Not for me, of course. I'm doing it for that damned wife of mine."

I smiled.

He asked me to help him screw a pair of hinges onto a door. When I was preoccupied with the job, he started talking to me gently.

"Gregory?"

"Yeah?"

"So, they tell me you're going to

boarding school?"

(Silence.)

"You don't want to go?"

(Silence.)

I said nothing. I didn't want to cry like a baby.

Grandad took the wooden panel from my hands and set it aside. He put his hand under my chin and turned my head towards him.

"Listen, Toto. Listen to me. I know more than you think I do. I know how much you hate school, and I also know what goes on at home. Well, not exactly, but I can guess. I mean with your parents... I don't suppose every day is a barrel of laughs."

I made a face.

"Gregory, you must trust me. I'm the

one who thought of boarding school, and who planted the idea in your mother's head. Don't look at me like that. I think it'll do you good to get away for a bit, to see other things. You're suffocating at home with your parents. You're their only child – they have only you and they see life only through you. They don't see how much damage they're doing by investing absolutely everything in you. I promise, they've got no idea. Actually, I think the real problem is elsewhere. If you ask me, they should start by resolving their own relationship before worrying so much about their son. I ... oh no, Gregory, please don't cry, I didn't mean to upset you, I just wanted to ... oh, to hell with it! I can't even put you on my lap, you're too big now!"

"I'm not upset, Grandad, it's just water overflowing."

"Never mind then ... come on, it's all right. Let's pull ourselves together. We have to finish this sideboard for Joseph if we want to eat for free at his restaurant. Here, pick up your screwdriver."

I blew my nose on my sleeve.

Then, in the silence that followed, just as I was about to start work on the second door, he added, "One last thing, and I won't mention it again. But what I want to say is important. I want to tell you that if your parents argue, it isn't because of you. It's their problem and they are the only ones to blame. You've got nothing to do with it – nothing at all, got it? And I guarantee that even if you were top of the class, if you got nothing but As and Bs, they would still fight. They'd just have to find another excuse, that's all."

I didn't reply. I slapped the first coat of varnish onto Joseph's sideboard.

7

When I got home, my parents were going through school brochures and tapping away on a calculator. If life was a comic strip, there would have been a bubble of black smoke above their heads. I said goodnight and headed for my room, but they stopped me in my tracks.

"Gregory – come here, will you?"

From the tone of his voice, I guessed that my dad was in no mood for jokes.

"Sit down."

I wondered what they were cooking up for me this time.

"You know your mother and I have decided to send you to boarding school..."

At last! I thought, Something you agree on. About time. Pity it's about something so stupid!

"I imagine you're not too happy about it, but that's the way it is. We're at a dead end. You do nothing at school, you've been expelled, nobody wants to take you, and the local school is a disaster. We don't have much choice. But what you probably don't realize is that it's very expensive. We want you to know that we're making a sacrifice for you – a big sacrifice."

I laughed silently. Oh, but you shouldn't have! Thank you, thank you, you really are too kind. Allow me to kiss your feet!

Dad continued. "Don't you want to know where you'll be going?"

(Silence.)

"You don't care?"

"Nope."

"Well, actually, we've got no idea. Your mother has spent the whole afternoon on the phone with no result. We have to find a school which is prepared to take you halfway through the year, and which—"

"There's where I want to go," I said, interrupting him.

"Where's 'There'?"

"There."

I held out the leaflet with the photo of the students at the workbench. My mum put on her glasses.

"Where is it? Thirty kilometres from the Welsh border ... Granfield Technical College ... but they only have a sixth form."

"No they don't."

"How do you know?" asked my dad.

"I phoned."

"You?"

"Yes, me."

"When?"

"Just before the holidays."

"Really? You actually phoned them? But why?"

"I just did ... to find out."

"So?"

"So nothing."

"Why didn't you tell us?"

"Because it's impossible."

"Why impossible?"

"Because they only accept students with good school records. Mine's terrible! It's so bad it scares the paper it's written on."

My parents said nothing. My dad read the Granfield prospectus, and my mum sighed.

The next day I went to school as usual, and the next day, and the day after that.

I began to understand the expression "to blow a fuse".

It was exactly that. I had blown a fuse. Something in me had dimmed, and everything left me cold.

I did nothing. I had run out of ideas. I didn't even want to have ideas. I put all my Lego in a box and gave it to my cousin Simon. I watched TV all the time. I gaped at miles of video tape. I lay on my bed for hours on end. I did no building. My hands hung limply by my skinny sides. Sometimes I felt like they were dead. They were just about OK for pressing the buttons on the remote, or popping open a can of Coke, but that was all.

I was no good. I was turning into an idiot. My mum was right; soon I'd be eating hay like an animal.

I didn't even feel like going to my grandparents'. They were nice enough, but they didn't understand. They were too old. Anyway, how could Grandad

Leo really understand my problems? He'd always been a genius. He'd never had any problems.

As for my parents, forget it. They didn't even talk to each other any more. A couple of total zombies. I stopped myself from doing something – anything – to shake them up once and for all, to get some kind of reaction. Though what that might be I didn't know.

A word, a smile, a gesture.

Anything.

I was flaked out in front of the TV when the phone rang.

"So, Toto, have you forgotten me?"

"Erm ... I didn't feel like coming over today."

"What? What about Joseph? You promised to help me deliver the sideboard!"

Oh no. I'd completely forgotten.

"I'm on my way. Sorry!"

"No problem, Toto. No problem. It's not about to run away."

Joseph treated us to a slap-up meal to say thank you. I had a steak the size of Mount Vesuvius, with all the trimmings; mushrooms, onions, chips, salad. Mmmm, delicious. Grandad Leo smiled at me.

"It's good to see you eating like that, Toto. Lucky your old ancestor works you hard now and again so you can eat like a pig."

"What about you? Aren't you eating?"

"Oh, I'm not that hungry. Your grandmother stuffed me full of breakfast as usual."

I knew he was lying.

After lunch we visited the restaurant kitchen. I couldn't believe the size of the pots and pans; they were enormous. And there were huge ladles, giant wooden spoons and dozens of razor-sharp knives arranged in rows from biggest to smallest.

"Hey, meet Titch!" Joseph shouted. "Our new recruit... He's a good lad. We're going to work on him, give him a chef's hat, and in a few years' time those imbeciles from the Michelin Guide will be swooning all over him, you mark my words! Say hello, Titch."

"Hello."

Titch was peeling millions of potatoes. He looked pretty happy. His feet
had disappeared under a mountain of
peelings. When I looked at him I
thought, He must already be sixteen,
lucky bloke.

When he dropped me in front of the
house, Grandad Leo said again, "Right,
so you'll do what we said, won't
you?"

"Yeah, yeah."

"Don't worry about the mistakes, or
the style, or your terrible handwriting.
Don't worry about anything. Just tell
them how you feel, all right?"

"Yeah, OK."

I started that very night. I must have

cared more than I admitted, because I did eleven rough drafts. Even so, my letter was not a long one.

I'll show you:

To the Headteacher of Granfield Technical College.

Dear Sir,

I would like to go to your college, but I know that it is impossible because my school record is too bad.

In your brochure, I noticed that you have workshops for mechanics and carpentry. You also have computer labs and greenhouses etc.

Personally, I think that good marks are not all there is to life. Motivation is just as important.

I would like to go to Granfield because I'm sure I would be happy there. At least I think so.

I am not very big: I weigh about 35 kilos of hope.

Goodbye,

Gregory Murray

PS: This is the first time I have ever begged someone to let me go to school. I think I must be ill.

PPS: I am sending you the plans of a banana peeler that I built when I was seven.

I read it over and found it quite creepy, but I couldn't face doing it again a thirteenth time.

I imagined the headteacher's face

when he read it. He was bound to think, So who is this joker? and then crumple the letter into a ball and aim straight for the bin. I didn't feel like sending it, but I'd promised Grandad Leo and I couldn't get out of it now.

I posted it on the way home from school. It was when I was having my snack that I re-read the brochure and saw that the "Dear Sir" headteacher was in fact a "Dear Madam". What a moron! I thought to myself, biting my lip.

35 kilos of hope? 35 kilos of hope-less, more like!

Then it was half-term. I went to Yorkshire to my mum's sister, my aunt Suzie. I played on my uncle's com-puter, never went to bed before midnight, and got up as late as possible – which was when my little cousin jumped on my bed shouting, "'Ego! Do 'ego? Geggry, will you come and do 'ego with me?"

For four days I built with Lego. I made a garage, a village, a boat. Every time I finished something, my cousin was as excited as could be. He would stare at it in admiration and then... *Wham!* He would hurl my creation on the floor with all his might, smashing it into a thousand pieces. The first time it really annoyed me, but when I heard him laugh I forgot about all the time I'd wasted. I loved hearing him laugh. It fixed my broken fuse.

My mum came to pick me up at the station. Once we were in the car, she

said, "I've got two things to tell you –
one good and one bad. Which shall I
tell you first?"

"The good."

"The head of Granfield phoned.
She's considering you, but first you
have to take some kind of test."

"Ugh! That's what you call good
news? A test? What am I supposed to
do with a test, make paper planes? So
what's the bad news?"

"Your grandad's in hospital."

I knew it. I was sure of it. I had felt it
in my bones.

"Is it serious?"

"They don't know. He fainted, and
they're keeping him under observa-
tion. He's very weak."

"I want to see him."

"No. Not yet. No one can see him for the moment. He has to get stronger first."

Mum was crying.

8

I took my grammar book to revise on the train to Granfield, but I didn't open it. I didn't even pretend. I was incapable of putting one thought in front of the other and making my brain work. The train passed miles of gigantic electricity poles, and at each one I murmured, "Grandad Leo ... Grandad Leo ... Grandad Leo ... Grandad Leo ... Grandad Leo ... Grandad Leo ... Grandad Leo." Between the pylons I said silently, "Don't die. Stay here.

I need you. Gran needs you too. What would become of her without you? She'd be so miserable. And what about me? Don't die. You can't die, you've got no right. I'm too young. I want you to see me grow up. I want you to be proud of me. My life is just beginning. I need you. And if I get married one day, I want you to see my wife and children. I want my children to go into your workshop. I want them to know the smell of it."

I fell asleep.

9

In Wales a man came to meet me off the train. During the trip to the school I found out that he was the gardener of Granfield – "the groundsman" as he called it.

I was pleased to be in his van. It smelled of diesel oil and old leaves.

I had dinner in the canteen with the boarders. They were all big hefty lads. They were nice to me and told me loads of stuff about the school: the best places to hide for a smoke; how to get on the cook's good side to get extra rations; the way into the girls' dorm through the fire escape; the obsessions of various teachers and all that.

They laughed loudly. They were stupid. But friendly stupid. Stupid like lads together. Their hands were covered in cuts and grazes, with black grease under the nails. They asked me why I was there.

"Because no other school wants me."

That made them laugh.

"Not one?"

"Not one."

"Not even the reform school?"

"Nope," I said, "not even the reform school. They thought I was a bad influence."

One of them clapped me on the back. "Welcome to the club, mate!"

Then I told them about the test I had to do the next morning.

"So what you doing still up then? Go and get your brainy sleep!"

I couldn't get to sleep. I had a weird dream. I was with Grandad Leo in a fantastic park, and he was driving me up the wall. He kept tugging at my clothes saying, "So where is it, the place they hide to smoke? Ask them where it is."

At breakfast I couldn't swallow a thing. My stomach was like lead. I had never had such a pain in my life. I was breathing fast. I was in a cold sweat. I was boiling and freezing at the same time.

They sat me down in a small class-room and left me alone for a while. I thought they'd forgotten me.

Then a woman gave me a big test booklet to fill in. The lines danced before my eyes. I didn't understand anything. I put my elbows on the table with my head in my hands. I needed to breathe, to calm down, to empty my head. Suddenly, I was staring at the graffiti carved into the table. There was one bit that said "I like big boobs" and another next to it: "I prefer span-ners". That made me smile, and I got down to work.

At first it was OK, but the more pages I turned, the fewer answers I knew. I began to panic. The worst was a paragraph a few lines long. The instructions said: "Find and correct the errors in this text." It was awful. I couldn't see a single mistake. I really was the stupidest person on the planet. The thing was full of mistakes, and I couldn't even see one! I had a lump in my throat. It came higher and higher, and my nose started itching. I opened my eyes wide. I couldn't cry. I wasn't going to cry. I WASN'T GOING TO, d'you hear?

And then it came anyway. A great big tear plopped itself right in the middle of the test booklet. I gritted my teeth as hard as I could, but I could tell I was about to crack. I knew the dam was going to burst.

It had been too long. Too long that I'd held back from crying, stopped myself thinking about things. But there comes a time when it all has to come out, all that messy stuff you keep hidden at the back of your brain, way back in the deepest recesses of your mind. I knew that once I started to cry, I wouldn't be able to stop. Everything would rush out at once; Big Doggy, Marie, all those years at school when I'd been bottom of the class. Always the village idiot. My parents who didn't love each other any more, those endless miserable days at home, and Grandad Leo in his hospital bed with tubes up his nose and his life seeping slowly away.

I was on the verge of sobbing, biting my nails to the quick, when I heard a voice saying, "Come on, Toto, what are you playing at? What's going on here? Would you mind not dribbling all over your pen? You'll drown it if you go on like that."

So there you are. Now I was really cracking up! *Hey, you up there – this is a mistake! I'm not Joan of Arc, hearing voices. I'm just a little nobody in a big mess!*

"All right Mr Self Pity, let me know when you've finished making a scene. Then maybe we can get some work done."

What was going on? I looked around the room to see if there were any hidden cameras or speakers. What the *hell* was going on? Had I ended up in the twilight zone or what?

"Grandad Leo, is that you?"

"Well who d'you *think* it is, the Pope?"

"But ... how come?"

"How come what?"

"Er ... how come you're here, speaking to me like this?"

"Don't talk rubbish, Toto. I've always been here and well you know it. Right, that's enough messing around. Now concentrate. Pick up your pencil and underline all the adverbs... No, not that one, you can see it's an adjective. Now, find the subjects of the sentences... Right, draw arrows to point them out... Good. Now, *think!* Find all the prepositional phrases you can... There, look at the preposition, and there's its object, that's right. Check everything. You see, you can do it if you concentrate. Now go back to the last page. I saw some dreadful mistakes in your maths. They made my hair stand on end. Go on, the division, yes, do that one again. *Again!* Look, you've forgotten something. That's it, and now let's look at page 4, please."

I felt like I was in a waking dream, totally concentrated, yet without the slightest stress. I was writing in a fog. It was the strangest sensation.

"There you are, Toto. I'm leaving you now. It's time for the essay, and I know you're better at that than I am. Yes you are, honestly. So I'm leaving, but just check your spelling, all right? Do the same as before, little arrows and check everything. Pretend you're a word policeman – ask every word for its ID before you let it go: 'You there! What's your name?' 'Noun, sir.' 'But there are lots of you: so what are you?' 'A plural noun, sir.' 'OK, so what do you need?' 'An S, sir.' 'Right, off you go.' You see what I mean?"

"I think so," I replied.

"Please don't talk aloud!" exclaimed the supervisor. "You must work in silence. I don't want to hear a word."

I read over what I'd written. At least fifty-seven times. Then I gave in my booklet. Once I was in the corridor, I whispered, "Grandad Leo, are you still there?"

No reply.

I tried again on the train on the way home.

Nothing.

When I saw my parents' faces on the station platform, I knew something had happened.

"Is he dead?" I asked. "He's dead, isn't he?"

"No," said my mum, "he's in a coma."

"Since when?"

"Since this morning."

"Is he going to wake up?"

My dad made a face, and Mum collapsed against my shoulder.

10

I didn't go to see him in hospital. Nobody did. It wasn't allowed, because the slightest germ could kill him.

But I did go to my gran's, and I got a shock when I saw her. She looked even more frail and fragile than usual, like a little white mouse engulfed by her blue dressing gown. I was standing like an idiot in the middle of the kitchen when she said, "Go and work a little, Gregory. Get the machines working. Touch the tools.

Feel the wood. Go and talk to his stuff. Tell it he'll be back soon."

She was crying noiselessly.

I went into the workshop and sat down. I crossed my arms over the bench, and at last I let myself cry.

I cried all the tears that I'd been holding back for so long. How long did I stay like that? An hour? Two? Maybe three?

When I stood up I felt better, as if I had no more tears left to cry, no more misery inside me. I blew my nose on an old glue-stained rag lying on the floor, and that's when I saw the words I had carved into the wooden bench the time I was expelled:

HELP ME.

11

I got into Granfield.

I didn't feel especially good or bad about it. I was just pleased to get away, to "get some fresh air" as Grandad Leo would have said. I packed my bag and didn't look back when I closed the door to my room. I asked my mum to put Mr Martin's money into my savings account. I no longer felt like spending it. I no longer felt like doing anything, except for what was impossible. And I understood that not everything in life could be bought.

My dad took advantage of one of his long-distance rounds to drive me to my new school. We both realized that from now on we would be going our separate ways.

"Call me if you hear anything, OK?"

He nodded, then gave me a clumsy hug.

"Gregory?"

"Yes?"

"No. Nothing. Try to be happy – you deserve it. You know, I've never said this, but I think you're a good lad ... a really good lad."

And he hugged me hard before getting back into his car.

12

I wasn't the best in the class, I was even one of the worst; if I think about it, actually I think I was at the bottom. But the teachers seemed to like me.

One day, Mrs Vasey, the English teacher gave us back our essays. I had 6 out of 20.

"I hope your banana-peeling machine worked better than this," she said with a little smile.

I think they liked me because of that letter I'd sent. Everyone here knew that I was a rubbish student, but that I wanted to do well.

On the other hand, in drawing and technology I was king. Especially in technology. I knew more than the teacher. When the others couldn't do something, they'd come to see me before they asked him. At first Mr Joyce didn't like it, but after a while he started doing it as well, which was quite funny.

My worst thing was PE. I'd always been bad at it, but here it showed even more because the others were all really sporty – and what's more, they loved it. I was terrible at *everything*. I couldn't run or jump or dive or catch a ball, let alone throw it. Nothing. Zero. Bottom of the heap.

The others made fun of me, but in a friendly way. They would say, "Hey Gadget-Boy, when you going to invent a muscle-building machine?"

Or, "Watch out lads! Murray's gonna jump. Get the bandages out!"

My mum called every week. At first I'd ask her if there'd been any news. One day she finally exploded.

"Listen Gregory, stop! Stop asking me that. You know perfectly well that if there were any news I'd tell you straight away. I'd rather hear about you, about what you're doing, your teachers, your friends, all that stuff..."

I had nothing to say to her. I forced myself a bit, and then I cut off the conversation. Anything that wasn't about my grandad didn't matter.

13

I was OK, but I wasn't happy. I was frustrated at not being able to do anything to help Grandad. I would have moved mountains for him, cut myself into little pieces and fried myself up for dinner. I would have picked him up and carried him to the ends of the earth. I would have done absolutely anything to save him, but there you are, there was nothing to do but wait.

It was unbearable. He'd helped me when I needed it most, but what could

I do for him? Nothing. Nothing at all.

Until the infamous PE class.

That day, it was rope-climbing. For me this was the absolute worst. I'd been trying since the age of six, and I'd never managed it. Not once. The knotted rope was my greatest shame.

When it came to my turn, Millsy shrieked out, "Come and see! Gadget-Boy's gonna try the rope!"

I looked to the top of the rope and murmured, *"Grandad Leo, listen to me. I'm going to do it. I'm going to do it for you. For* you, *d'you hear me?"*

At the third knot I was ready to give up, but I gritted my teeth and pulled on my pathetic scrawny arms. Fourth knot, fifth knot… I was about to let go. It was too hard. No, I couldn't give in,

I had promised! I gulped, and pushed on my feet. It was no good, I'd never make it.

That's when I saw them down below, all the lads from my class in a circle. One of them shouted, "Go on, Gadget! You can do it!"

So I tried again. Drops of sweat blurred my vision. My hands were on fire.

"Gad-get! Gad-get! Gad-get!" they chanted to encourage me.

Seventh knot. I had to let go.

Down below they were singing, "Go Gadget, go go go!"

They certainly gave me strength. But not enough.

There were only two knots left. I spat in one palm then the other.

Grandad Leo, here I am. Look! I'm sending you my strength. I'm sending you my willpower. Take it, take it all! You need it. The other day, you sent me your knowledge. Well now I'm sending you everything I've got; my youth, my strength, my breath, my determination, my puny little muscles. Take it, Grandad! Take it all, I beg you!

The skin inside my thighs began to bleed, and my joints were completely numb. But only one more knot to go.

"Go on, Gadget! Gooo ooon! *Gooooo ooooon!*"

The boys were going crazy. The teacher was shouting loudest of all. I yelled *"GRANDAD, WAKE UP!"* and grabbed the top of the rope. Below, celebration broke out. I was crying tears of joy mixed with tears of pain. I let myself slide, half falling to the floor. Millsy and Sam caught me and hoisted me into the air yelling, "GAD-GET! GAD-GET! GAD-GET!" Everyone in the gym was cheering.

I fainted.

From that day on, I was a changed man. I became determined, tough. I had a will of iron. I had drunk the magic potion.

Every evening after lessons, instead of going to watch TV, I went walking. I went through villages, crossed woods and fields. I walked for hours, breathing slowly and deeply and always thinking: *Take all this, Grandad, breathe in this air, breathe. Smell the earth and the grass. I'm here. I'm your lungs, your breath and your heart. Relax, take it all.*

It was mouth-to-mouth by long distance.

One evening my mum phoned. When the supervisor came to get me, my heart sank.

"I've got bad news, sweetheart. The doctors are stopping the treatment. It's doing no good."

"You mean he's going to *die*?" I yelled into the receiver for the whole corridor to hear. "Why don't you just switch him off? That way it would be quicker!"

And I hung up.

From that day on, I stopped pre-tending. I went back to playing table football with the other kids, I worked badly and hardly spoke to anyone. Life disgusted me. In my mind, he was already dead. When my parents called again, I hung up on them.

Then yesterday a sixth-former came to get me. I was in bed fast asleep. He shook me hard.

"Wake up, mate!"

My mouth was all gummed up.

"Whash happening?"

"Are you Toto?"

"What? Why?"

I rubbed my eyes.

"Because there's this old bloke downstairs in a wheelchair, and he's shouting that he wants to see his Toto... He wouldn't by any chance mean you, would he?"

Wearing just my boxers, I sprinted down the four flights of stairs, already sobbing like a baby.

He was there by the canteen door, with a paramedic next to him holding a drip thing.

Grandad Leo was smiling at me.

As for me, I was crying so much that I couldn't even manage a smile.

He said, "You should do your flies up, Toto. You'll catch cold."

And at that, I smiled.